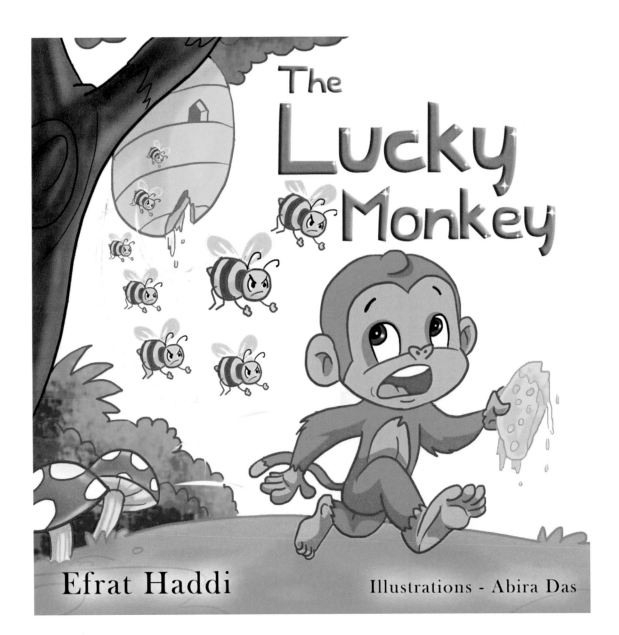

The Lucky Monkey

Efrat Haddi

Illustrations - Abira Das

The Lucky Monkey

Written by Efrat Haddi
Illustrations by Abira Das

Copyright c 2014 by Efrat Haddi

First edition – 11/2014

Tanya was a monkey who lived with her family in the jungle of Africa. She had a son whose name was Troy.

Troy was the most mischievous monkey in the whole jungle.

Everyone called him a lucky monkey because he was always getting into mischief and yet, he never got hurt.

On Sunday, Troy climbed up a banana tree to get some bananas.

He hung onto the banana cluster and rocked it from side to side.

Suddenly, the banana cluster broke away from the tree. Troy fell down from the tree and all the bananas fell on his head, one by one.

"Troy," said Tanya. "Are you alright? You were lucky you didn't hit your head any harder. Don't rely on luck only and please, think before you act."

"Oh Mother," said Troy. "I'm the lucky monkey, nothing will ever happen to me."

On Monday, Troy saw a beehive in a tree trunk.

He reached out and tried to get some honey from the hive.

The bees became angry. They chased him away and they almost stung him.

"Troy," said Tanya. "I am glad you are alright. You were lucky that you weren't stung. Don't rely on your luck only and please be careful. Think before you act."

"Oh Mother," said Troy. "I'm the lucky monkey, nothing will ever happen to me."

On Tuesday, Troy sneaked up behind a zebra while she was eating grass in the field.

He pulled the zebra's tail and fled. The zebra was frightened. She kicked up her back legs and she almost kicked him.

"Troy," said Tanya. "I am glad you are alright. You were lucky that you weren't kicked. Don't rely on your luck only and please be careful. Think before you act."

"Oh Mother," said Troy. "I'm the lucky monkey, nothing will ever happen to me."

On Wednesday, Troy saw a hippo that was sleeping. The hippo was not feeling well and was cold.

Troy put a flower up to the hippopotamus' nose and when the hippo smelled the flower, the pollen made him sneeze. He almost sneezed all over Troy.

"Troy," said Tanya. "I am glad you are alright. You were lucky that you weren't infected. Don't rely on your luck only and please be careful. Think before you act."

"Oh Mother," said Troy. "I'm the lucky monkey, nothing will ever happen to me."

On Thursday, Troy decided to cross the river. There were lots of crocodiles in it. The crocodiles were poking their heads out of the water.

Troy jumped from one crocodiles head to another.

One crocodile opened his mouth and almost swallowed Troy.

"Troy," said Tanya. "I am glad you are alright. You were lucky that you weren't eaten. Don't rely on your luck only and please be careful. Think before you act."

"Oh Mother," said Troy, "I'm the lucky monkey, nothing will ever happen to me."

On Friday, Troy climbed the banana tree again to get some bananas.

Just like before, he hung on the banana cluster and rocked it from side to side.

Suddenly the cluster of bananas broke away from the tree.

Troy fell to the ground but this time the banana cluster fell on his head.

Troy was hit very hard and was in a lot of pain.

"That's very strange," thought Troy to himself. "Today I had no luck. I will probably get lucky again tomorrow."

On Saturday, Troy went back to the beehive that was in the tree trunk.

Just like before, he reached into the hive to try to get some honey from it.

This angered the bees and this time they chased him and they did sting him.

Troy was in a lot of pain. "It's even stranger," thought Troy to himself. "Today I also had no luck. I will probably get lucky again tomorrow."

The next day, Troy sneaked up behind the zebra while she was eating grass in the field.

Just like before, he pulled the zebra's tail and fled. The zebra was frightened and she kicked her back legs.

This time she kicked Troy and he was flung to the other side of the field.

He was in a lot of pain. "What's going on here?" thought Troy to himself. "I had no luck again today. I will probably get lucky again tomorrow."

The next day, Troy saw the hippo sleeping again. The hippo was very sick.

Just like before, Troy put a flower up to the hippopotamus' nose and when the hippo smelled the flower, the pollen made him sneeze.

This time the hippo sneezed all over Troy and Troy did become infected and became very ill.

"Mother," said Troy. "I think you were right, I shouldn't rely only on luck. I should be careful and think before I act."

"That's right," said Tanya. "Sometimes we are lucky and sometimes we are not. Therefore we should always be careful and think before we act and not rely only on luck."

When Troy recovered, he decided to cross the river again.

He could see the crocodile's heads sticking out of the water.

"I must be careful and think before I act rather than rely solely on luck," he thought.

After thinking, Troy decided to cross the river somewhere else, somewhere where there were no crocodiles.

He was able to cross the river safely.

Since that day, Troy didn't rely on only his luck. Instead he thought carefully before acting.

Sometimes he found he was still a lucky monkey.

A Note from the Author

To my dear readers:

Thank you for purchasing "The Lucky Monkey"

I really enjoyed writing it and I've already had some great feedback from kids and parents who enjoyed the story and illustrations. I hope you too enjoyed it.

I appreciate that you choose to buy and read my book over some of the others out there. Thank you for putting your confidence in me to help educate and entertain your kids.

If you'd like to read another book of mine , I've included it on the next page for you.

Sincerely yours

Efrat Haddi

More GREAT books by Efrat Haddi

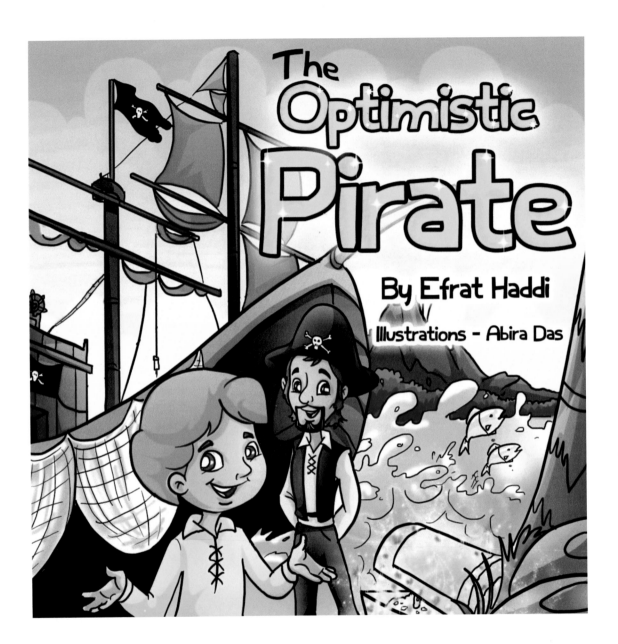

The Optimistic Pirate

By Efrat Haddi

Illustrations - Abira Das

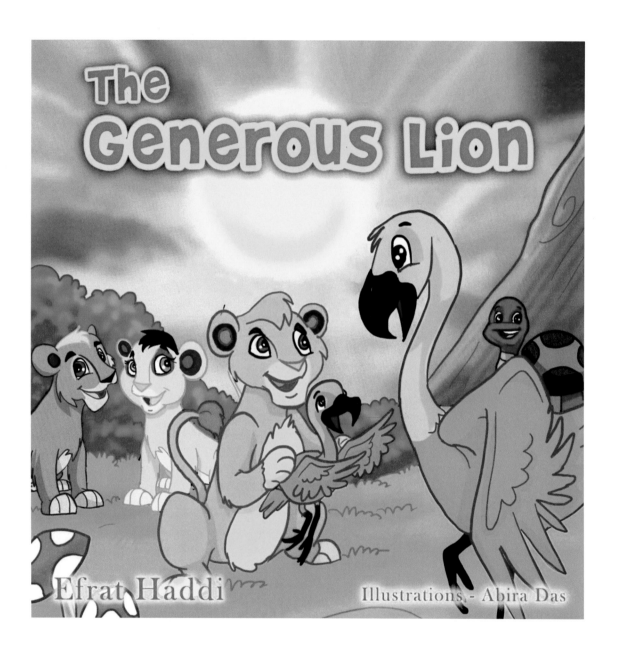

The Generous Lion

Efrat Haddi

Illustrations - Abira Das

The
RESPONSIBLE Lion

Efrat Haddi   Illustrations - Abira Das

The Sharing Lion

Efrat Haddi

Illustrations - Abira Das

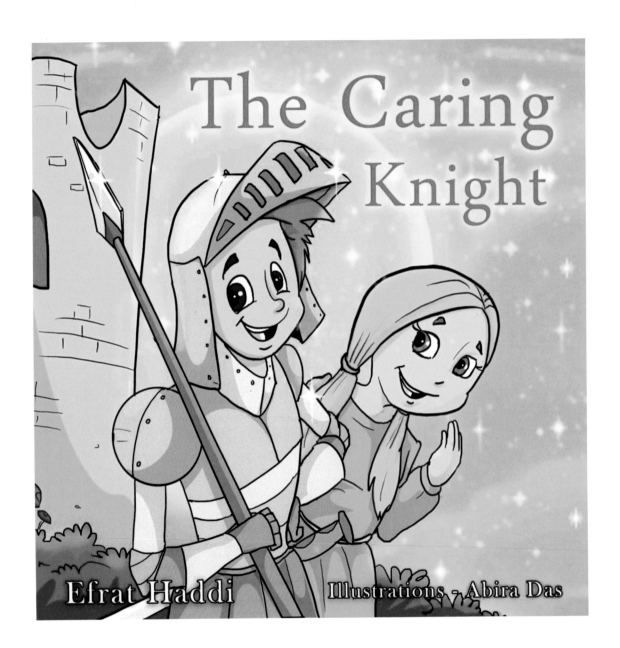

The Caring Knight

Efrat Haddi

Illustrations - Abira Das

The Persistent Owl

Efrat Haddi   Illustrations - Abira Das

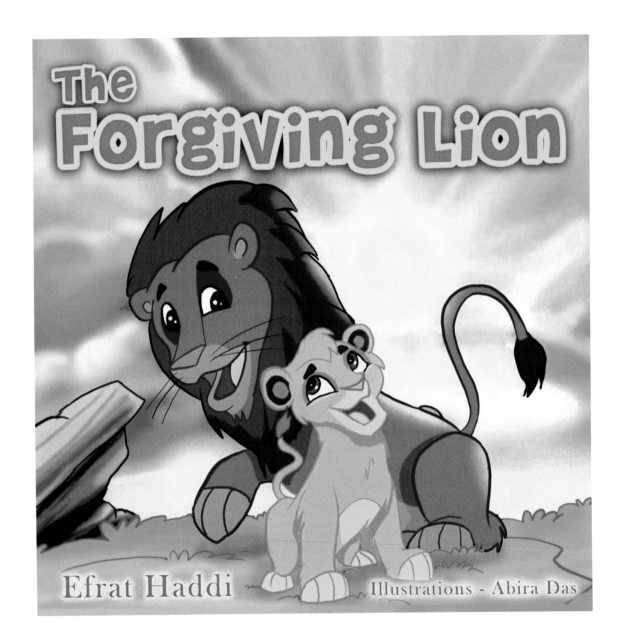

The Forgiving Lion

Efrat Haddi   Illustrations - Abira Das

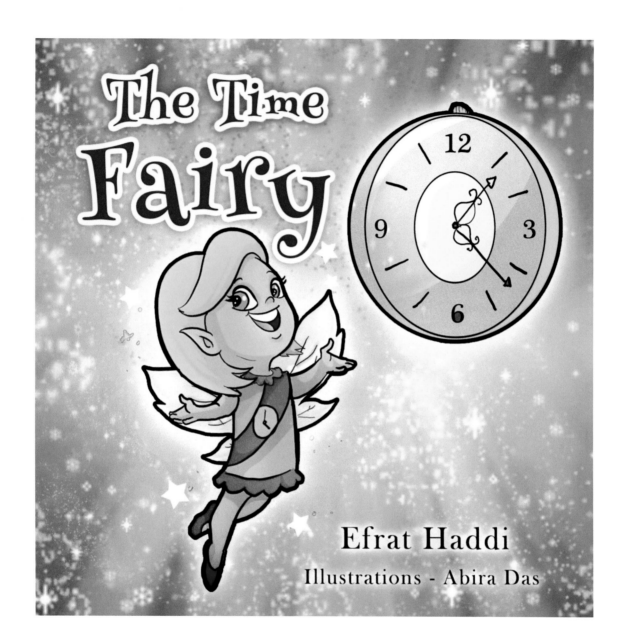

The Time Fairy

Efrat Haddi

Illustrations - Abira Das

THE DRAGON
IN ME

Efrat Haddi   Illustrations - Abira Das

Lily's Shy Parrot

Efrat Haddi

Illustrations - Abira Das

Magic Seeds
of Patience

Efrat Haddi

Illustrations - Abira Das

Magic Seeds
of Patience

Efrat Haddi
Illustrations - Abira Das

Lily's Shy Parrot

Efrat Haddi
Illustrations - Abira Das

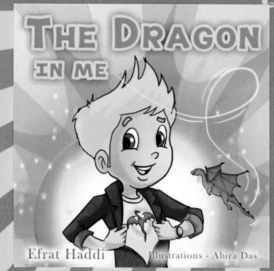

THE DRAGON
IN ME

Efrat Haddi   Illustrations - Abira Das

The Time
Fairy

Social Skills for Kids
Collection

. Das

Made in the USA
Lexington, KY
22 September 2017